ALIEN ROAD

ALIEN ROAD

M.J. McISAAC

ORCA BOOK PUBLISHERS

Published in Canada and the United States in 2021 by Orca Book Publishers.
orcabook.com

Library and Archives Canada Cataloguing in Publication
Title: Alien road / M.J. McIsaac.
Names: McIsaac, M. J., 1986- author.
Series: Orca currents.
Description: Series statement: Orca currents
Identifiers: Canadiana (print) 20210093668 | Canadiana (ebook) 20210093676 |
ISBN 9781459826984 (softcover) | ISBN 9781459826991 (PDF) |
ISBN 9781459827004 (EPUB)
Subjects: LCGFT: Novels.
Classification: LCC PS8625.I837 A79 2021 | DDC jc813/.6—dc23

Library of Congress Control Number: 2020951460

Summary: In this high-interest accessible novel for middle readers,
thirteen-year-old Ridge goes on a boat trip through the legendary Bermuda Triangle.

Orca Book Publishers is committed to reducing the
consumption of nonrenewable resources in the making of our books.
We make every effort to use materials that support a sustainable future.

Orca Book Publishers gratefully acknowledges the support for
its publishing programs provided by the following agencies: the
Government of Canada, the Canada Council for the Arts and
the Province of British Columbia through the BC Arts Council
and the Book Publishing Tax Credit.

Edited by Tanya Trafford
Design by Ella Collier
Cover artwork by Ella Collier
Author photo by Crystal Jones

Printed and bound in Canada.

24 23 22 21 • 1 2 3 4

For Jess

Chapter One

"Would you stop that?"

Ash jumps off her beach chair, frowning at the freckled boy in khakis and golf shirt sitting in the sand between us. Karl Barrington. He's been digging a hole with his popsicle stick and flicking sand everywhere since he sat down.

"Sorry," he grumbles.

"You're not sorry at all," snarls Ash, wiping sand off her legs.

I roll my eyes and try to focus on my sketchpad. My drawing of Wraith—a wicked-looking masked super villain of my own creation—is only halfway done. It's for my graphic novel. My dad convinced me to start one over Spring Break. Said it would be good to try and make a story out of all these characters I'm always coming up with. I want to finish it before the vacation is over so I can show him when I get home. But with Ash and Karl around all the time, it's hard to focus.

"I said I was sorry," Karl snaps. "Why would I say it if I didn't mean it?"

"Because you're still doing it!" Ash shrieks, pointing at the sand Karl keeps flicking out of his little hole. "Ridge, make him stop it!"

"I don't know why you think I have that power," I tell her.

"He listens to you."

I look over at Karl, sitting in the sand. We've been at Juneberry Beach two whole days and the kid still hasn't put on a bathing suit. Just the same designer khakis and various colors of identical golf shirts. I didn't know they were designer, but Ash did. Ash is a label girl. She loves labels. Especially the kind that seem to be plastered all over Karl and his family. She knows what kind of sunglasses Karl's dad wears, and what kind of purse Karl's dad's girlfriend Gina carries around. She's impressed by their shoes, watches, even their luggage. And she talks to me about it. All. Day. Long. I don't know why she thinks I care. None of it means much to me. But I do know that labels like those mean Karl's dad is rich. Filthy rich. How a guy like Karl's dad became friends with my mom and Ash's mom, I'll never understand.

Karl stares at me, as if expecting orders.

"Knock it off, Karl," I say. "I'm sick of listening to Ash whine."

With a horrified *guh* noise, Ash kicks the sand, sending it flying into my face. It's in my eyes, my nose, my mouth. I taste the hard, salty grains grinding on my tongue. I spit. Beside me, Karl laughs.

By the time I blink away all the grit, Ash is storming back to the house. Her house. The one she lives in with her mom, Jes. I can see her sitting on the deck with my mom and Karl's dad and his girlfriend. She waves to Ash and Ash's arms flail wildly. I don't know what she's saying, but I know she's not telling them anything good.

All four of them turn and look in my direction. Mom frowns.

"Great," I mutter.

As soon as Mom gets ahold of me, I know she is going to lecture me about being nicer to Ash.

Jes is Mom's friend from university. She invited me and Mom to come visit her for Spring Break. Sounded all right to me—a week in the Florida Keys with lots of time to draw, and maybe even some time on a jet ski. And I heard that Jes had a teenage daughter. *Cool,* I thought, *Spring Break with a high-school girl.* But then that high-school girl turned out to be Ash—whiny, boring, mean old Ash.

"She hates me," says Karl.

"Yeah," I nod, spitting out more sand. "She hates me too. At least you get to leave soon."

Karl's face goes kind of funny. His mouth twists to one side, like he isn't so happy about that either.

"What?" I ask. "I'd sure rather be out on your fancy boat than stuck here with Ash."

Karl shrugs and looks down at the sand hole. "You can have my spot."

I laugh. "Don't tease me, Karl. I'd take your place in a second."

I mean it. Like I said, Karl's dad is filthy rich. The only reason he's even in Florida is because the private yacht he chartered for Spring Break launches from here. Then they're off to sail the Caribbean in luxury. *Chartered.* I learned that word recently too.

Fancy rich people don't rent things. They charter them. Karl told me there's even a Jacuzzi onboard. And some kind of inflatable slide thing that they can set up if they want to. He told me it goes from the top deck down into the ocean. I don't even know what that would look like. But I know it sounds awesome.

Karl doesn't smile. Just stares down miserably at the sand.

"What's the matter?"

"It's not safe," he says.

"What isn't? The boat?"

He shakes his head.

"What then?"

He looks at me, his mouth twitching. I think he's deciding whether or not to say. Finally, he speaks again. "Do you know how we're getting to the Caribbean, Ridge?"

"Awesomely?"

"No!" Karl says, waving his hand at me. "Not awesomely. *Dangerously*."

"Dangerous how?"

"Don't you know where we are?" Using the popsicle stick, he draws what looks like the southern tip of Florida in the sand. He adds some of the islands of the keys branching off. "*This* is where we are. Now look here, the Bahamas." He makes a bunch of dots a little further south of Florida. He makes another dot to the left of that. "Puerto Rico." Then a bit to the north he makes another dot. "Bermuda."

I'm impressed. I definitely didn't know my geography that well when I was ten. Heck, I'm thirteen and I still don't know it that well.

"Okay?" I say, not sure what any of this is supposed to mean.

Karl scoffs. He draws a line from Florida, along the Bahamas, to Puerto Rico. Then another line up to the Bermuda. And one more line, back to Florida.

A triangle.

"It's the Bermuda Triangle," Karl whispers.

I can't help it. A laugh bursts out of me. I brush the sand off my sketchbook. "The Bermuda Triangle? That's not real, Karl. That's just an urban legend."

He scowls. "No, it isn't!" He jumps to his feet, pointing at the sand. "Do you know how many boats have disappeared in this area? Countless! I've read all about it!"

"Okay, Karl," I say, trying to get a hold of my laughter. "Maybe your dad should hire the coast guard to protect your floating mansion from aliens or ghosts or whatever you think is out there."

"No one knows what's out there," he says. "That's why it's so dangerous!"

I shake my head and go back to my drawing. The hood of my Wraith character looks smudged. *Great.* I try to rub the smudge out but I only make it worse.

"Dang." I've been working on this character for two weeks, and now I've gone and smudged it. Correction. Ash and her angry sand kicking smudged it. How am I supposed to fix it now? Am I going to have to start all over again?

Karl stomps his foot. "Ridge, you're not even listening to me!"

"Listening to what?" I snap. "I'm sorry, Karl, but it's hard for me to feel bad about you and your luxury boat cruise. Being afraid to go on a trip like that because of the Bermuda Triangle is the most ridiculous thing I've ever heard."

He doesn't say anything to that. But his chin starts to quiver. Now I feel like a real jerk.

Before I can apologize, he takes off running for the house. Oh no. Did I make him cry? I didn't mean to. I was just upset about my drawing.

I risk a glance over my shoulder and see that Karl's given up on running. It's not easy to do on sand. He struggles, bursts of sand flying up behind his flip flops. I spot Ash on her way back to the beach. She's got a smile on her face now, so big and so wide that I can see her braces. I've already learned that she hates to show her braces.

"Ridge!" she squeals. "Ridge! Guess what?"

I've never heard Ash say my name like that. Never so...happy. "What?" I ask.

"We're going!" she says, throwing her arms up. "Karl's dad invited us, all of us! We're going to the Caribbean!"

Chapter Two

The *Paradise II* isn't a boat. It's a sea hotel. I stand on the dock beside Ash, staring at the four-story, gleaming white luxury cruiser with my jaw hanging open.

"Oh my..." Mom stands behind me, her hands resting on my backpack. "Jes, are you sure this is the right boat?"

"Yeah."

He nods, thinking about it for a minute. I feel my cheeks getting warm. "Sweet name, champ," he says.

"Thanks," I reply and leave Captain Bob alone on the dock. I stand beside Mom as Mr. Barrington emerges from a staircase above us.

"So, what do you think, kids?"

"Oh my god," says Ash, beaming. "Mr. B, this is so amazing!"

"Really, Eric," says Mom. "This is incredible."

Gina appears on the banister beside him. She's wearing a gold bikini, her face covered by gigantic sunglasses. "You've only seen the bow!" she laughs. "Eric, they need the grand tour."

"I can do that," offers Captain Bob.

Ash's eyes light up. Gross. She's looking at Captain Bob like he's the latest iPhone.

"Yes." Gina claps her hands, a delighted grin on her face. "First stop, the bar. What's a tour without a little refreshment?"

"Oh," says Jes, smiling at Mom. "I'm sure it's five o'clock somewhere."

Mom laughs and she and Jes head up the stairs with Mr. Barrington. I watch Ash position herself so she's walking side by side with Captain Bob.

"She says that all the time," says Karl.

I hadn't noticed him there. He is standing on the opposite staircase. "What?"

"Jes," he says. "*It's five o'clock somewhere*," he repeats, his voice high-pitched. "What does that even mean?"

I shrug.

For a while, there's an awkward silence. I notice the rhythmic sound of water hitting the dock.

"Do you want to come see your room?" Karl says, finally. "You can drop off your bag."

I slip my bag off my back and let it hang loose on one shoulder. It is kind of heavy. "Okay."

I follow Karl up the stairs to the second level. It's like we're aboard some kind of fancy dinner club.

A covered deck looks out on what would be wide-open ocean once we get going. Two white leather corner couches sit on either side of the deck, with embroidered pillows and matching white coffee tables. And beside the stairs lies what looks like a giant bed, divided into three sections. For working on your tan, I guess.

A goofy grin spreads across my face. "Karl, this is siiiiiiick."

Karl doesn't smile. In fact, he seems pretty indifferent to all of it.

"Your room is this way," he says, disappearing through a narrow door.

The narrow hallway is also pure shining white. I'm afraid to touch anything and make it dirty. After a few steps it opens up into a living room bigger than my entire house.

"This is crazy!" I say, plopping down on the plush gray couch. At least this room isn't so white. There's matching gray chairs and more couches lining the tinted windows on either side of the room. And a flat-screen TV the size of my bedroom wall looms over everything. A dining-room table for eight is in the corner, set for what looks like a five-course dinner.

Karl watches me from another doorway, waiting to lead me deeper into the ship. He looks annoyed.

"Are you coming?"

"Uh, yeah," I say, pushing myself out of the cushy pillows. "Sorry, I've just never been on a boat this fancy before. Guess you're used to it."

Karl shrugs. "No. This is my first time too."

Another couple turns down narrow halls and Karl shoves open a door. "In here," he says.

I let out another laugh. It's bigger than any room I've ever had. It has a bathroom and everything. A huge flat-screen TV on the wall and two decent-sized beds. And a desk in the corner. With a laptop and maps strewn across it.

"I've taken the far bed," says Karl. "So you can have this one. It's close to the bathroom."

"What? I'm sharing with you?"

"Yeah," he says, jumping on his bed. "It'll be fun."

Fun. Considering the kid hasn't cracked a smile since I got here, I seriously doubt that. Still, better than sharing a room with Mom. I drop my backpack on the bed. Officially mine.

The TV is on, stock images of Caribbean fun-in-the-sun fade in and out in a slideshow. "Do we get satellite?"

"Yeah, a few channels. Lots of movies."

That's good.

I take a closer look at the computer on the desk. "Is there WiFi on this boat?" I ask. A webpage is open—"Bermuda Triangle Mysteries." About thirty more tabs in the browser.

Karl leaps over his bed and slams the lid closed and frowns at me. "This is my laptop. It's private."

"Are you researching the Bermuda Triangle?"

"What do you care?" he snaps. I notice his cheeks are flushed.

"C'mon, let me see." I make a move toward the desk again. Karl shrugs and falls back onto the bed.

I open the computer and glance at the article.

"It's a list," Karl says.

"List of what?" I scroll through, dates and names of people. There are hundreds of them.

"Of ships and planes that disappeared."

The list goes all the way back to 1918. Warplanes and cargo ships, entire crews lost at sea. "This is pretty dark stuff, Karl."

He folds his arms across his chest. "Yes, you think I'm silly. You've made that clear."

His cheeks have turned a shade of tomato now. I remember how he had started to cry yesterday when he first told me about the Bermuda Triangle. I figured he was just being a baby. I didn't realize he was scared enough to research it. "I don't think you're silly," I say, looking back at the screen. "I just think you've let your imagination make a big deal out of nothing. Everyone knows the stories about away at his laptop. And I can't believe I want to join him. I want to get on that computer and read what he's reading. I want to know exactly what happened to the *Paradise*. I wipe the beads of sweat pooling on my forehead. It can't be what Karl thinks. The Bermuda Triangle isn't a real thing. It isn't. There was a perfectly good explanation for why the *Paradise* disappeared, and it didn't have anything to do with the Bermuda Triangle. Because the Bermuda Triangle was a myth...wasn't it?

Ash blinks a lot at Captain Bob, her giant eyes slathered in black eyeliner. When did she find the time to put all that goop on her face? Captain Bob does not appear to notice.

"How's that sound, Reg?" asks Captain Bob, looking at me.

"My name is Ridge," I say, glad to have a reason to not have to answer the question. I haven't been listening to a word he's said.

Captain Bob's smile fades a bit, and he shifts from foot to foot. "Ah, sorry, man. Ridge, right. Ridge."

Ash glares at me.

"Well, Ridge," says Bob, slapping Chef Andres on the back. "Like I said, Andres is happy to fix you up anything, at any time of day, so don't hesitate to put in your order, even if it's pizza at midnight. All right, champ?"

Champ again.

One of the attendants, Penelope I think, leans forward, smiling. "You just let me know if you need anything too," she tells me.

Mom laughs and rubs my head. "Well, I don't think he'll be needing any midnight pizza, don't worry."

I pull away from Mom, annoyed that she is treating me like a kid.

"But it's vacation time!" says Bob, throwing open his arms. "No rules on vacation, isn't that right, Mr. B?"

Mr. Barrington stands over the mini bar, lifting his martini shaker to the air. "That's right, Bobby! No rules on vacation! In fact, Ridge," he points at me, "I *insist* that you and Karl indulge in midnight pizza at least twice this week."

The crew bursts into laughter, the kind of laughter Ash uses for Captain Bob. Too much. Totally fake. I guess you have to when the guy making the joke is the guy signing the paychecks.

"All right," says Captain Bob, clapping his hands together. "Let's get this vacation started!" Penelope and the other attendant Dana let out a couple high-pitched *woohoos* and Ash joins them, following after Captain Bob like a puppy. Mom and Jes push themselves up off the couches and head over to the bar with Mr. Barrington and his girlfriend.

Karl stays where he is, staring at his laptop. I join him, squishing in beside him on the stairs.

"Find anything?" I ask. "About the *Paradise*, I mean."

He hands the laptop to me so I can see the article he's reading.

Billionaire Gambling Tycoon Feared Dead

After Private Yacht Disappears

I scan the article, and the hairs on the back of my neck start reaching for the sky.

Famous party billionaire Nelson Moore went missing while enjoying his summer vacation off the coast of Barbados last month. A distress call was received by officials at 11:11 p.m. on November 11th, from Moore's private yacht, the Paradise. The charter company, Elegance Cruises, has stated that Captain Jeff Curry radioed for help after his instruments mysteriously began to fail. Sources describe the final message from Captain Curry as disturbing. "We don't know where we are. The waves are glowing. The sky looks green in color. All of this is wrong." After that, the vessel disappeared from all radar. Search efforts so far have not yielded any clues as to the fate of the Paradise and its passengers. Officials fear we may never know.

I blink at the screen, my mouth suddenly dry.

"See?" says Karl. "Believe me now?"

"There's got to be an explanation," I tell him. "Did you find anything else?"

"Not a lot," he says. "Mostly articles about this Moore billionaire person and what they did with all his stuff."

"Karl!"

We both look up and see Mr. Barrington watching us. "Take Ridge up to the bridge," he says. "Help Captain Bob get this floating tub on her way, eh?"

Karl frowns. "I don't want to have anything to do with getting this doomed voyage started."

His dad rolls his eyes. "Ridge, don't let Karl scare you. The boy didn't want to go skiing in the

Alps because he was worried about Yetis. And we were fine, weren't we, Karl?"

Karl frowns harder. "This is different!"

"Go on up, Ridge," says Mr. Barrington, "I think you'll find it very interesting. Don't let Karl keep you from the fun."

Karl turns his scowl on me, like he's daring me to listen to his dad instead of him. I want to listen to his dad. Karl is only ten. And paranoid. *Yetis in the Alps?* How embarrassing. And the Bermuda Triangle is probably just as cringe-worthy.

But still. The *Paradise* did go missing. This article is proof it wasn't just a rumor.

Mom waves me over, but I'm not done with Karl yet.

"What about Captain Bob?" I whisper to him.

Karl's frown melts away, confusion on his face instead. "What about him?"

"He's Captain of the *Paradise II*," I say. "He must know what happened to the *Paradise*. He works for the same company that Captain Curry worked for, doesn't he?"

Karl nods, "Elegance Cruises."

"Maybe he can tell us what happened."

"So do you want to go up to the bridge? See what we can find out?" Karl asks.

I do. Because the goose bumps on my skin aren't going away. And I'm starting to feel as nervous as Karl.

Suddenly the floor beneath my feet starts to vibrate. The engines.

The *Paradise II* is already heading out to sea.

Chapter Four

Karl and I climb our way to the bridge. It looks like something out of a sci-fi movie. You'd think we were launching into outer space, with all the screens and buttons and monitors. Massive windows surround the room, offering a 180-degree view of the ocean ahead of us.

Captain Bob stands in front of the screens. He's pointing at a sonar-looking thing, trying to explain it to Ash. Ash, sitting in a swanky leather captain's chair, beams back at him.

"Have a seat, guys," says Bob when he sees me and Karl standing awkwardly by the door. He motions to a cream leather booth and polished coffee table set up on a platform against the wall. Karl hops up, bouncing on the cushions. I join him. We're seated right behind the captain's chair. The stunning blue of the water beyond the glass seems to be asking us to jump in.

Penelope swoops in beside Karl, "How about a drink, boys?" Her smile is friendly.

"I'll have a margarita," says Karl, eyes narrowed on Captain Bob.

Penelope nods. "Your favorite."

"What? You're only ten, Karl! You can't drink."

Penelope laughs. The sound reminds me of a wind chime. "Don't worry, Mr. Ridge. I'll make sure they hold the alcohol."

Karl rolls his eyes at me. "It's just a fruit slushy."

"Can I get one for you, Mr. Ridge?"

"You can just call me Ridge," I reply.

"Ridge it is," she says with that perfect smile.

I nod and I guess she takes that as a yes to the margarita. She disappears to go make our drinks.

"And over here," Captain Bob is telling Ash, "we can keep an eye on the weather. See that?" He is pointing at one of the screens. "Sunny skies and clear sailing. A perfect start to the voyage."

"What happens if these break down?" Karl hops out of the booth and shoves his way between Bob and Ash to look at the computer screens.

"Oh, you don't have to worry about that, champ. They haven't failed me yet."

"But they could," Karl challenges. "It's just like any computer and computers break, don't they?"

"Karl," snaps Ash, "don't be so annoying."

I try not to laugh at the look on Captain Bob's face. Karl's questions have flustered him, and it's clear Bob isn't sure how to handle it. He starts explaining something about the software, but I'm not listening because Penelope has returned. She is carrying two giant goblets of green slush. Blazing red cherries and bright yellow pineapple garnish the rim. She places them down in front of me and winks. There's a glint from her necklace. The pendant is a bright blue stone with squiggles carved into it. It's mesmerizing.

She notices me looking and wraps her hand around it.

"Uh, I like your necklace," I say, reaching for one of the goblets.

"Thanks. It's been in my family forever. It's for protection."

"Protection?"

"Good luck. Smooth voyage, that kind of thing. My family always taught me that a true explorer can never be too careful around these parts."

"Why's that?"

She lowers her voice, conspiratorially. "Because there is a great power living beneath these waves."

"A great power? What do you mean?"

She laughs. "It's just a superstition. How's your margarita?"

I take a quick sip, the sugary ice exploding with a sweetness that makes me wince. "It's awesome," I lie.

Penelope smiles at me before Bob's laughter calls her attention to his conversation with Karl.

Karl is not laughing. In fact, it's clear he doesn't think there's anything funny about what he said.

"You're a real sharp kid, that's for sure," says Bob. "But the navigation systems on the *Paradise II* are a bit more professionally calibrated than what's on your laptop or tablet, champ. Don't sweat about them breaking down. The *Paradise II* is brand new, top of the line."

Karl frowns. "That's what they said about the *Titanic*."

"Karl!" I say, surprised he just used the T-word.

"What?" he says. "They did say it! And what about the first *Paradise*? Was it top of the line too?"

I choke, the bluntness of Karl's question forcing lime slush down the wrong tube.

From the looks of it, I'm not the only one who's surprised. Penelope is standing absolutely still now, her hand clasping the blue stone of her necklace again. Captain Bob's champ-guy grin has turned into a frown. Karl stares up at him, not at all bothered by the reaction he's just caused.

"The instruments on the *Paradise* failed," Karl continues. "Why would that happen? And why wouldn't it happen to us? Huh?"

"You've been reading about the *Paradise*?" Bob asks.

Karl nods.

Bob looks out the windows, leaning over the monitors, his foot tapping at the floor like he's trying to think of what to say.

Penelope just keeps fiddling nervously with her necklace. Her eyes are welling up. And that's when the realization hits me.

"Did you know them?" I ask quietly. "The crew, I mean?"

Penelope nods, her eyes closing.

"Captain Curry was my first boss," says Bob, still looking out the windows. "He was a really great teacher and friend to me."

I suddenly feel like a real jerk for agreeing to come up here with Karl. We've just opened up what I should have realized would be a painful subject. The *Paradise* was a ship full of Penelope and Captain Bob's friends.

"We were all hit hard by what happened," says Penelope.

"But what *did* happen?" asks Karl. I see Ash reach out and pinch him. He cries out, but I'm glad she did it. *Shut up, Karl.*

Captain Bob breathes in deeply through his nose before pushing back from the desk. "Look, I don't want you guys to worry about that. The *Paradise* was an older ship, and I'll bet there were a lot of factors that contributed to its disappearance, including having too many guests aboard. Anyway, you shouldn't be up here getting bored by all this technical stuff. Why don't you head to the deck and relax? This is supposed to be a vacation."

Bob ushers Ash and Karl to the door. I follow, leaving my barely sipped slushy on the table. Once we're outside, Bob closes the door with a loud slam. Karl and I are left facing a scowling Ash.

"What is your problem?" she growls.

Karl is offended. "My problem? What's *his* problem? Don't we have a right to know what we're facing? Don't we need to know about the dangers that are out there? We are heading into the Bermuda Triangle!" His elbow nudges mine. "Tell her, Ridge."

Ash's dagger-eyes snap to me. "The Bermuda Triangle?"

"I...uh..." I don't want to admit that I let Karl convince me we should talk to Captain Bob. But I don't have to because my stammering is enough for Ash. She reaches out and smacks me on the head.

"You're both losers. The Bermuda Triangle? Are you *serious*? Do you have any brains at all? You really upset the Captain, and for what? Some ridiculous superstition?"

My insides shrivel to nothing. Ash is right. Penelope had been really upset too. She looked like she had been about to cry. And it's all my fault. I should have stopped Karl.

Ash smacks me again. "You got me kicked out of there when I was trying to learn about the boat!"

"Oh please," says Karl. "You just wanted to flirt with Captain Bob."

Ash's eyes flare and I brace myself for another blow. Instead she turns away, her purple hair flying in our faces as she storms off down the deck.

I don't know what to do. Part of me wants to go back inside and apologize, tell Penelope and Captain Bob how sorry I am about what happened to their friends. But I don't think either of them want to look at me or Karl right now.

Karl sighs. "I guess we'll just have to keep researching on our own."

"What?"

"Well, Captain Bob's not going to help us. He just wants to sweep the whole thing under the rug. If we're going to find out what happened to the *Paradise*—"

"Stop, Karl! Don't you realize how much you upset them?"

"I just asked the question!"

"It was rude."

"Rude? Who cares about rude? Our lives are at stake!"

I feel like ripping my hair out. "I shouldn't have let you talk me into this. Look Karl, Ash's right. The Bermuda Triangle isn't a real thing."

"It is so! You saw the list of ships!"

"But there could be a hundred different reasons why those ships disappeared! Normal, legitimate reasons! Bad weather, crazy currents, drunk drivers! Who knows?"

"All in the same spot?"

"Karl, I'm done. Don't talk to me about this anymore, ok? We have to let it drop."

He opens his mouth to fight me, but I walk away before he can. I'm not sure where to go though. Ash's probably telling my mom and the others what happened. I don't want to see them and their looks of disappointment. And I have no idea how I'm going to face Penelope and Captain Bob again. I'm so embarrassed and mad at myself. Maybe I should just hide out in my room for the rest of the trip.

Chapter Five

The clock on my bedside table says 2:30 a.m.
I haven't been able to sleep at all, thanks to the guilt
I still feel. Mom didn't say anything to me, but Karl's
dad gave him a harsh lecture about getting his
head out of the clouds and growing up. Karl refused
to talk to me after that, locking himself in our room
to do more research until he had to come out for

dinner. And that was awkward. He sat across from me, giving me a death stare for the whole meal.

There's an angry grumble from my stomach. I'm starving. I barely ate anything at dinner. Mostly because I didn't want to. Not just because I was feeling too crummy, but the spread was pretty gross. There were nuts in everything, even in the salad, which I didn't understand. Why would you put nuts in salad? And for the main course we had crab, which I always thought was a fancy people food, but now I know it's just gross. Mom and the others tore into the shells like wild animals, pieces of pink crusty exoskeleton flying all over the place, in my hair and onto my plate. The only food that wasn't weird was my little pile of lemon rice, and it got so splattered from all the flying crab juice that I didn't want it anymore.

It didn't help that Penelope was the one who served us dinner. She seemed different. Less smiley than when we first met her. And I hated that I had a part in making that smile stop.

There's a lot of rustling from Karl's side of the room as he turns over for the hundredth time. He's been tossing and turning all night. I'm pretty sure he's still awake. Probably itching to get back to his research.

Penelope said the waters here were special somehow. I wonder how she'd feel if she knew that Karl thought her special waters were cursed.

That's it. I can't lie here anymore, hating Karl, thinking about Penelope and what jerks she must think we are. I grab my sketchbook and pen and creep my way out the door, leaving Karl to continue his restless sleep.

I'll draw on the deck. That'll be nice. I'll start a new sketch under the moonlight. That should keep my brain occupied.

But once I'm alone in the dark hallway, I wonder how relaxing this will actually be. There's something creepy about a boat at night. It's eerily quiet. The only sound is the low hum of the engines and the pad of my feet on the floor. The lights that line the hallway are dim. Their artificial yellow glow gives way to the silver of the moon when I finally make it outside onto the deck.

I sit down on a plush-looking couch and flip open my sketchbook. The crisp moonlight reflects off the page exactly the way I like it to. The light bounces so brightly I could practically use the paper as a flashlight. It makes me feel like the moon's a fan of my drawings, trying to get a good look at what I'm working on.

I flip past my drawing of Wraith. I took a class at the start of the summer—it was all about drawing comics. And line work. About how the weight of the lines are important to how an image reads. I worked so hard on the lines for Wraith. Thick ones where he was more in shadow, thinner where the light was hitting him. It took forever. And now, he's smudged. All that work for nothing. It's time to start something new. Something for the moon, maybe. Since it's watching.

I breathe in the smell of the water, fresh, light and warm, as my pen moves over the paper. I'll draw the man in the moon. Someone to keep it company up there. I feel better already, and I'm so glad not to be lying awake in bed anymore. Before I know it, the strokes are starting to make a shape—not a man, but a girl. A girl like Penelope. With hair tied back in a long ponytail just like hers. The smile is the most important part, and when I start, I'm worried I'm not getting it right. So I move down to the neck, where I've started the shape of her necklace. I etch in the curves and lines of the carving on the blue stone as best as I can remember them. Squiggles, three of them. Like the letter S laid on its side, one on top of the other. And three dots.

"Ridge?"

I jump at the sound of my name, and when I do, my hand slips.

"What are you doing?"

Karl is standing behind the couch, looking over my shoulder at the drawing he's just ruined.

"You scared the life out of me Karl! What are you doing?"

"I couldn't sleep."

I frown at the thick black line that I've just slashed across Penelope's face. "Well, you screwed up my drawing. Thanks for that."

"You were the one holding the pen."

He takes a seat on the couch across from me, and lies back, looking up at the stars. "I've seen that symbol before."

"What?"

"That symbol you were drawing. The one on the necklace. Where did you see it?"

"Penelope's necklace. Same as you."

He sits up then, suddenly interested. "But that's not where I saw it. You're saying Penelope was wearing this symbol?"

"Yeah. It's on her pendant. So what?" I wish Karl would just go away and leave me to my sketching. "What are you talking about, Karl?"

"I've seen that symbol before. In the stuff I've been reading. My research."

"Karl, what did I say about leaving me out of this crazy Bermuda Triangle thing?"

He springs up off the couch and reaches for my sketchpad. But I am too quick for him and pull it out of his reach. "No, Karl. You're letting yourself get carried away."

"Just let me see it!" he cries.

I hand it to him, afraid he's going to wake everyone else up.

He studies the page, his tight grip crumpling the paper. "Yes! I've seen this! It's on the banner of this website I've been studying."

"That's great, Karl. Can I have my drawing back, now?"

"Why do you think Penelope has this necklace?"

"I don't know, she said it's a family heirloom or something. Who cares?"

"I think the website said it's somehow related to the Bermuda Triangle. It's a symbol that is supposed to protect people from the bad stuff."

"Karl, *give it*." I lunge for my sketchbook but he leaps back. Something inside me snaps. I'm furious that he won't drop this whole Bermuda Triangle madness, that he's crumpling the paper, that he wouldn't let me draw in peace, that he managed to suck me into his conspiracy theories in the first place. I lunge again. Karl can see how mad I am now. He scrambles off down the deck, and I chase after him. Our bare feet quietly smack the floors as he flies down the stairs to the lower level. I follow and fling myself around the first corner only to slam right into Karl. The two of us fall to the ground.

"Karl, give me—" Karl covers my mouth and points down the deck. I can see someone huddled on the ground by the bow.

It's Penelope.

She looks like she's scrubbing the deck. Which is weird. It's like three in the morning.

Karl gets back on his feet and wedges himself in the doorway to the dining room. He waves at me to join him, and without thinking I do. I'm not really sure why I do, but I'm not really sure why Penelope is scrubbing floors in the middle of the night either. It all just feels *off*.

Penelope finally stands up. She reaches for the arm of the massive outdoor couch—it's been pushed back from its usual spot—and gives it a shove. She has to use her whole body against it, but she finally manages to put it back in the right place. And then she starts walking our way.

"Go go go!" whispers Karl frantically, opening the door to the dining room and pushing me inside.

We plaster our backs to the wall on one side of the doorway. Penelope enters the dining room too but marches right by us. She didn't even notice us! She pushes through the doors that lead into the kitchen. And she's gone.

"Come on," says Karl, heading back out to the deck.

I follow him to the couch. With considerable effort, we manage to nudge it out of place again so we can get a look at what Penelope was doing to the floor beneath it.

There on the sun-bleached wood is a character scribbled in bright white chalk. The same symbol I'd seen on her necklace.

I stare dumbly at Karl whose creased forehead makes me think he has a better idea of what we are looking at than I do.

"What—What does this mean?" I ask him.

"It means," says Karl, "that Penelope knows *exactly* what we need to be afraid of out here."

Chapter Six

Back in our room, Karl pulls up the website he was
talking about. I sit beside him on his bed. And there it
is, in the top left corner of the screen—the symbol on
Penelope's necklace, the same one she drew on the
deck. My eyes scan the headline of the main article
on the home page—*Walking Procyon's Road.*

"What is this?" I ask him. "What's a procyon?"

"I had to look it up too," Karl says. He reads a definition from a bookmarked page. "*Procyon is one of the brightest stars in the sky and part of the Winter Triangle, along with Betelgeuse and Sirius.*"

"So it's a star. But what does that have to do with that weird protection symbol?"

"Well, I only just started reading up on it, but basically the inhabitants of the Procyon system were looking to create a new colony in a new solar system," Karl said. "They sent out hundreds of exploration missions. One of their ships, it's believed, came here to Earth…"

"Wait a second," I said. "Are you seriously talking to me about extra-terrestrials? A spaceship full of star people?"

"I know how it sounds! But listen to this." Karl reads from the article. "*The Procyon Pilgrims arrived and left before the birth of humanity, their settlement begun, but never completed. The evidence of their* existence can be seen beneath the waves of the North Atlantic—a massive winding stone path known to some as Procyon's Road."

Karl scrolls through a series of satellite pictures. I can see some straight, grid-like shadows faintly visible on the ocean's floor. It's pretty convincing, but it has to be a trick of some kind.

"But be warned." Karl continues. "No man who has set out to travel along Procyon's Road has lived to talk about it. Rumor has it the sacred ruins are still protected by the power of the Procyon Pilgrims." Karl looks at me. "That must be what happened to the first Paradise! That's what's making the ships disappear!"

"Karl, this is an alien conspiracy website," I say. "It's just some nutcase talking about visitors from another planet. There has to be a more legit resource out there—"

I stop as one of the images Karl scrolls past catches my attention. It's a black-and-white photograph of a group of smiling people on the deck of a sailboat. The year 1925 is handwritten in the corner.

I recognize one of the people. So does Karl.

"Is that *Penelope*?" Karl asks.

I squint my eyes, like that's going to change what I'm looking at. There is no doubt in my mind that it is Penelope. And she is wearing that same necklace with the blue stone.

"That's...that's impossible," I say weakly. And then I notice something else.

All of the people in the photograph are wearing the same necklace. *What the heck?*

"Oh, man. Listen to this," says Karl. He starts reading the article again. I just nervously pull at the tiny hairs on my arm. "*The power of the Procyon Pilgrims is to be respected and protected. All those who enter these waters ignorant of the forces hidden beneath the waves will meet their end. But those who mark themselves as believers of the Pilgrims* will be free to pass." Karl looks up, his eyes wide and his voice rising with excitement. "See Ridge? I told you, the symbol, it's for protection! It marks you as an ally."

I shush him. I'm not so much excited as confused. And worried.

"*We who revere the Procyon Pilgrims*," quotes Karl, "*hold steadfast to the faith that one day they will return to complete the mighty civilization they had only just begun. Mark yourself as friend, and you shall be seen as a true explorer.*"

"True explorer," I repeat, the words triggering a memory. "That's what Penelope said. That a true explorer can never be too careful. I thought she was just kidding around!"

"Do you think that's Penelope's grandmother or something in the picture?" Karl asks.

"Well, it's got to be some kind of relative, right? It looks just like her." *Just like her, I think.*

The resemblance is so identical it makes me uncomfortable.

"No kidding," Karl says, frowning at the screen. "Okay, so obviously Penelope knows about this Procyon power. That's why she marked the deck. She wants to make it safe for us to pass through."

I shake my head. "Alien powers? But that's impossible."

"You saw the satellite pictures. Something is definitely down there."

"They must be photoshopped," I insist.

Karl shrugs. "I don't know. Penelope seems to think it's true."

Penelope had seemed so normal. She couldn't really believe this stuff, could she?

"Either way," adds Karl. "I'm going to stay as close to that symbol as I can."

I'm starting to agree. Keeping close to the symbol might be a good idea—just in case. But still, my mind is racing. There has to be a reasonable explanation for all of this. But I can't come up with any.

Suddenly, a shrill scream makes both of us jump. It's a few seconds before I realize it's the alarm going off on the nightstand between our beds.

The big screen on the wall blinks to life, showing the current weather and the map that is tracking the ship's progress.

It's morning already.

"We're almost there," says Karl, eyes glued to the map.

"Where?"

"The triangle."

Chapter Seven

As I enter the dining room, the yellow morning sun streams in from the deck. Everything glitters and glows with the light of a new day. Through the open windows I can see Ash is already set up on a deck chair outside. Her sunglasses and earbuds block out the world. Mom and Jes are at the table. Their plates are piled high with a colorful fruit salad—pineapple, mango, cantaloupe and cherries. A platter of assorted buttery pastries and several pitchers of juice are on the table too. My stomach grumbles.

Karl pushes past me, grabs some fruit and a few pastries and marches out onto the deck. Through the window I see him plop down on a deck couch—Penelope's couch, the one with the symbol beneath it.

Mom waves me over. "Ridge! They've got sausage rolls. Your favorite!" She pulls out the seat next to her and starts loading sausage rolls on my plate. "Big as your arm. You won't believe…"

I sit down at the table, blocking out my mom's words, wondering about Karl. What's his plan? Is he just going to sit out there all day? What does he think is going to happen? If the ship goes down because of his aliens, does he think that being near the spot with Penelope's symbol is going to protect him?

My throat feels dry. *If the ship goes down….*

Penelope and the other attendant, Dana, breeze in with coffee and more juice for the table. How much juice do they think we can drink? Dana is all smiles and pleasant small talk. Penelope, though, seems different. She's more serious today. She looks tired.

As she leans over the table to top up Jes's coffee her necklace dangles out of her shirt.

"Oh, Penelope!" Jes exclaims. "That's beautiful! What is it? Lapis Lazuli?"

Penelope wraps a hand around the pendant. "Oh, no it's just a worthless stone."

"Ah ah ah," says Jes. "I am super into healing crystals. And I can tell you, there is no such thing as a worthless stone. Is it aquamarine, maybe? Calcite? It's calcite, isn't it?"

"No no." Penelope smiles. "It's nothing like that. It's just an old sea stone that's been passed down through the family. I just like it because it reminds me of them."

Sea stone. I can't help but wonder why she won't just say what it is. Just say it Penelope, *alien space treasure!* Then I shake my head. I hate that Karl has me believing his ridiculous theories! My throat feels dry again. I pour myself some pineapple juice and chug it down.

Jes can't let it go. She leans across the table for a better look at the necklace. "It's not raw sapphire, is it?"

Penelope laughs. "No, definitely not. Actually, the story in my family is that it came from a meteor."

I choke on my juice. Mom smacks my back and everyone looks at me. "I'm fine," I rasp between sputters. "I'm fine."

Jes leans her chin in her hands. "Oh, meteorite," she says, wistfully. "Now that is a very powerful kind of crystal. That must be why you emanate such a special energy. I felt it the first day we came onboard."

Penelope smiles thanks and leaves to clear some plates. *Special energy*. Jes has no idea.

"Ahoy, me hearties!" Mr. Barrington and Gina strut into the room. They are wearing matching white housecoats and slippers. "How are you all enjoying this fine day?"

Just then Captain Bob rushes in. He turns his back to the room as he speaks in hushed tones to Mr. Barrington.

Mr. Barrington frowns. "Instrumentation issue?" His voice is most certainly not hushed. "How serious is it?"

Mom and Jes quit shovelling food in their mouths. Gina freezes mid-scoop of fruit salad. I glance out at Karl—he's noticed Captain Bob talking to Mr. Barrington and put the tablet down.

"No no no, it's not a problem," Captain Bob is saying, a little louder now. "It's our policy to be transparent with our clients regarding the happenings of the ship. But it's not a serious problem. Everything is under control."

Ash has noticed Bob too. She sits up in her deck chair, pulls her headphones out of her ears and comes back into the dining room. "What's happening?" she asks. Karl is right behind her.

"Nothing to worry about, folks," says Captain Bob, flashing his movie-star smile. "Everything's fine, we should be coming up on Nassau by lunch. How does an afternoon of snorkeling sound?"

"I love snorkeling!" says Ash.

Captain Bob offers the room a double thumbs-up, and turns back to Mr. Barrington. "Sir, if you'll just come with me."

They leave together and everyone goes back to eating. Captain Bob's thumbs-up has satisfied them that everything is fine aboard the *Paradise II*. Everyone but me and Karl, that is.

Instrumentation issues. I'm not even sure what that is. I bet Karl's already looked it up on his tablet though. If it's a problem with the ship's computer systems, that could affect navigation couldn't it?

Karl's eyes meet mine. He points to the floor beneath him.

I pour another glass of juice.

Mom notices me chugging the fresh glass. She nudges my plate. "You haven't tried your sausage rolls."

"I'm not very hungry," I admit. The pineapple juice sloshes around in my gut. Captain Bob said everything's fine. But my skin feels hot with nerves.

Mom puts down her fork. She's got that worried face she always gets when I don't eat. "Honey, are you feeling all right? You look kind of pale." She presses her hand to my forehead.

"I'm fine, Mom," I say. "I just didn't sleep great."

"Look at the circles under your eyes," she says, frowning. "You look terrible. Maybe you should go lie down."

I think I should too. First hearing about Penelope's meteorite and then the instrumentation issues—I feel sick to my stomach. I leave Mom and the others to head back to my room. Even with the curtains closed, the room is still bright.

But the light is a dim, cool blue, and it calms the anxiety buzzing beneath my skin. I lay my head down on the fluffy white pillow and stare up at the big screen. The navigation showing our journey is pixelated and jittering.

That can't be good.

I turn over to face the wall. I think about Captain Bob's thumbs-up. It made Mom, Jes and Gina feel better. Because why would the ship's captain be throwing around thumbs-ups if we were in real danger?

But Mom and Jes and Gina don't know what I know. What Karl knows. Don't know about Penelope. And the old-timey picture. And her necklace.

They don't know about the Procyon Road.

Or that we are headed right for it.

I think about telling Mom. But I already know what she'll say—"Ridge, honey, you need to spend less time in your sketchbook and more time in the real world." Maybe she'd be right.

I cling to the thought of her laughing at me, of her telling me I'm being ridiculous. And I almost feel better. I tuck my arms under the pillow and try to get comfortable. And before long, I'm falling asleep, half-convinced everything is going to be okay.

Chapter Eight

That night, I have the worst nightmare of my life.
I stand on the deck of the *Paradise II*. It's late at
night. I don't know how late, exactly. I haven't looked
at a clock. But the moon is high. It glows a strange,
nuclear green. I've never seen the moon that color.
Like it's radioactive or something. It glints off the
water. The sea is calm, sparkling with the green.
Even the stars—too many to count—look green in

the dark sky. And then I hear a rattling sound. I look down at my hands and I'm holding a weird calculator thing. It's a Geiger counter. The numbers are ticking up as the rattling sound gets louder. Where did I get a Geiger counter? My palms start to sweat.

A wind picks up. It ruffles my hair, pulling me toward the water. In the sky, one of the stars is brighter than the others. It's getting bigger. How is it getting bigger? Because it's moving. A shooting star. And it's heading straight for the *Paradise II*.

I stare, mouth gaping, as the bright glistening star zooms toward me. Somehow I know it's a dream, but it's so bright, it's almost blinding. Then the light burns away, and I can see it for what it is—a giant hunk of space rock. It's cracked in a million places. And between the cracks, the green glow burns bright inside. Before I can scream, the rock slams into the water just in front of the *Paradise II*. The force of the impact slams me back against a wall. The boat rocks violently, water swamping the deck. So much water.

It pins me down. It's in my eyes. My nose. My throat. I cough and sputter, the swaying boat threatening to throw me overboard. I grab the rail. I cling there, waiting for the rocking to stop.

When it finally does, I let go of the railing. My dream self decides to go find Mom, make sure she's okay. But something moves beneath the waves.

I lean over the rail. Beneath the water's surface, I can see the meteor, its glowing green cracks are like a beacon on the ocean's floor. There's a shadow rising up to the surface. A person. It breaks the surface and swims for the boat. My stomach leaps into my throat as the person begins to climb. Straight up toward me. She hoists herself over the railing with ease. Now she's standing in front of me—sopping wet, glittering in robes of green stardust. The necklace with the Procyon symbol glows around her neck. Penelope.

She smiles at me and then looks back over the railing. I lean forward and see the meteor. It's growing beneath the waves. Fanning out and buckling over itself, stretching out across the ocean floor. It forms a glowing green road, reaching out into the abyss. And now I can see shadows. People. Standing on the ocean floor. They walk along the road. Headed for the *Paradise II*.

My voice catches in my throat. "Who are they all?" I squeak. "What do they want?" Penelope smiles again. "My family." She removes her glowing stone—meteorite, Jes called it—and places it around my neck. Then she kisses my cheek.

The shadows on the ocean floor move closer, and soon they are beneath the *Paradise II*. The ocean begins to boil and the ship starts to pitch. I'm tossed sideways. But Penelope doesn't seem to feel anything. She stands, unmovable. Like a statue.

There's a groan of metal. A crack of crunching hull. The ship is breaking up.

Water spills over the deck. It rushes in with a roar—the boat grinding and moaning under the pressure. The water is green, and glowing, just like everything else. It swallows me up—swallows the *Paradise II*. And the shadows are waiting. Penelope stands in front of them. Suddenly, the shadows rush me all at once, enveloping me in darkness.

I bolt up in bed. The world outside my window is dark. It's night. Have I been asleep all day? My body is covered in sweat. The nightmare is still fresh in my mind. My heart hammers in my ears. But that's all it was. A nightmare. My throat is dry and raw. Did I scream?

I need to drink something. All I can think about is that collection of juices from the breakfast table.

I glance over at Karl's bed. It's empty. It can't be that late. If it's night already, I've definitely missed snorkeling. Maybe I haven't missed dinner at least.

I make my way to the dining room. The halls are lit but it's quiet. Mr. Barrington usually blasts music all day. Mom and Jes can always be heard cackling with laughter. But right now, there's nothing. Not even the hum of the ship's engines.

Where is everyone?

There's a tingling in my skin. The echo of the Geiger counter from my dream sounds in my head.

"Hello?" The dining room is empty. There's no food out. No place settings. I must have missed dinner. I head out onto the deck. There's Karl, sitting on the same couch, with Penelope's symbol hidden beneath it.

"Karl!"

He looks up from his tablet.

"Where is everyone?"

He blinks at me, like he can't understand what I've said.

"Karl?"

His eyes go wide, like he's seeing me for the first time. He shakes his head. "Sorry, what did you say?"

"Are you okay?"

He thinks for a second. Finally he nods. "Yeah. Yes. Sorry. I think I just spaced out for a second."

"Have you been on that tablet all day?"

He nods. "Yeah, and I've discovered a lot of interesting stuff." He angles the device so that I can see. There's Penelope's symbol on the top left of the screen. "The pilgrims that were here? They left. Supposedly. But no one knows exactly *how* they left. And some people think—"

"Where is everyone?" The quiet is starting to freak me out.

"Hmm?"

"Where is everyone?" I ask for a third time. "My mom. Your dad. Ash. Where is everyone?"

"Oh..." Karl looks around. "Yeah, that's weird. I'm not sure."

"Did you guys have dinner?"

He thinks for a minute. "No....No, I don't think so."

"You don't *think* so?"

He frowns, confused. "I-I can't really remember.

The last thing I remember is having breakfast." He looks out over the water, the pale moon shining off the waves.

"Breakfast!?" I say. "Karl, that was hours ago! It's dark out!"

He leans over the couch and looks underneath, checking that the symbol is still there. Satisfied, he sits back up and puts his tablet down. "I agree, that's weird."

It's more than weird. The tingling in my arms races up the back of my neck. "Karl, I've got a bad feeling."

"Yeah," he says, getting off the couch. "Me too."

"They've got to be here somewhere, right? They wouldn't still be snorkeling."

Karl walks up to the railing and looks around the deck.

"Karl?" I say. "Didn't you guys go snorkeling?"

Karl doesn't answer. He's looking toward the bow of the ship. "Ridge," he gasps.

I join him by the railing and look to where he's pointing. I can see someone standing on the ship's bow. It's hard to tell from here but it looks like they're standing on the top rung of the railing.

It's my mom.

"Mom!" I call.

She's just standing there. Perfectly still on the topmost bar. Not balancing or anything.

"Mom!"

I run to her, Karl thumping along after me. "Mom, get down from there!"

She doesn't move. Doesn't even acknowledge me. When Karl and I are close enough to see her face, it's blank. She stares out at the night like a zombie—eyes empty, fixed on nothing.

"Mom? What are you *doing*?"

When she still doesn't move, I reach for her arm. "Mom?"

She gasps, like she's just come up from under water, and wobbles. She grips my arm with both hands and screams, nearly falling over. I pull back, as hard as I can. Mom topples off the railing and the two of us land hard on the deck.

Mom sits up, grabbing her heart. "Oh my goodness."

"Mom, what was that!?"

She grabs me in a hug. "I don't know. I must have—"

"What's going on?" From the upper deck, Mr. Barrington and Gina are looking down at us. Gina rubs her head. Mr. Barrington looks like he can't quite find his balance.

Jes pokes her head out of the dining room. Ash is with her. "Everything okay? We heard a scream." They both rub at their heads. Their eyes are puffy, like they just woke up.

Captain Bob appears beside Mr. Barrington. "Everything all right here, folks?"

"Fine," says Mom, getting to her feet. She dusts off her capris. "I must have been sleepwalking."

Sleepwalking? I've never known Mom to sleepwalk.

Ash folds her arms. "You're not supposed to wake a sleepwalker, Ridge."

"Okay, Ash," says Karl. "Maybe he should have just let her jump overboard then."

"Overboard?" says Mr. Barrington, alarmed.

"No no, I'm fine," says Mom. "Ridge just pulled me back from being too close to the edge. Thank you, honey. Everything is fine."

Too close to the edge is the understatement of the year. She was standing on top of the railing! But I can tell she doesn't want to freak anyone out, so I don't say anything. Karl keeps his mouth shut too, although he does glare at Ash.

"Holy jumpin' catfish!" exclaims Mr. Barrington, looking at his watch. "Where'd the day go? It's nearly 9:30! Did you guys have dinner?"

Mom and Jes shake their heads.

Mr. Barrington calls everyone inside, leaving me and Karl standing on the deck. The buzzing in my skin hasn't gone away. Whatever that was, it was very unlike Mom. And why was Karl so spaced out when I found him? Everyone, not just me, seemed to have lost track of the entire day. How was that possible?

"We must be getting closer," Karl says.

"What?"

"To the road."

I want to tell him to shut up, but I don't. Because all I can think about is my dream. About the road beneath the waves. And the shadows.

And Penelope.

Where *is* Penelope?

"It's going to get worse, you know," Karl says. "This is just the beginning. The closer we get to the road...the worse things are going to get. A lot worse."

"How long do we have?" I ask.

"If the instrumentation doesn't cause problems"—Karl shrugs—"then probably tomorrow."

Tomorrow.

I gulp. "I think that's enough internet reading," I tell Karl.

"Are you kidding?" he says. "It's all we've got!"

"It's not all we've got."

We've got Penelope.

Chapter Nine

I lie on my bed, bouncing a pair of rolled-up socks off the wall. Karl sits across from me, hunched over his tablet.

"What's taking so long?" he asks, anxiously.

I don't know. When Mr. Barrington and everyone sat down to dinner, Karl and I made an excuse that it was late and we wanted to watch a movie. Penelope had told me when we first got on the ship to let her know if we ever needed anything. So I asked Mom to ask Penelope to bring us a pizza.

That was the first part of the plan.

The second part was to get some answers from Penelope. If she ever showed up.

I glance at the clock in the bottom corner of the TV screen. We had ordered the pizza over an hour ago.

A knock sounds at the door.

Karl jumps to his feet.

As calmly as I can, I pull open the door.

And it's Dana, holding our pizza. "Special delivery!" she says.

I look back at Karl. His eyes bulge.

"Oh dear," says Dana, noticing the surprise on our faces. "Did I get it wrong? Your mom said pepperoni, right?"

I take the pizza. "Pepperoni's great, thanks." Dana hands me plates, napkins and cutlery. I guess rich people like to eat pizza with a knife and fork.

"Where, uh…" I stammer, "where's Penelope?"

"Poor thing," says Dana, "she's not feeling well. She's been holed up in her room all day."

"Oh," is all I can think to say.

"Can I get you boys anything else?"

I shake my head and she waves goodbye.

"'Not feeling well,' my butt!" Karl blurts out as soon as the door closes.

I throw the cutlery and stuff on the bed. "Keep it down Karl. She'll hear you."

"So what should we do now?"

I want to know what's happening on this ship. I want to know what's happening under the waves. I want to know why Penelope is painting weird symbols on the deck. And the only way to find out is to ask her.

I press my ear to the door and listen to make sure the hallway is clear.

"Come on," I say to Karl.

I open the door and we make our way to the deck.

I can hear Mom and Jes laughing in the dining room. Everyone's still at dinner. We tiptoe past them to a tiny hallway on the other side. Its dark, and it's tight. There's a bathroom and a broom closet. And at the end of the hallway is a stairwell to the lower deck—to the crew's quarters.

Karl stops. "We're not supposed to go down there," he whispers.

"You got a better idea?"

He thinks for a second. Finally he shakes his head and we head down the stairs.

It's bright down here, and smells like spaghetti. I can hear voices from the crew lounge. A figure moves across the door and I dive right, pulling Karl with me. We stand there, backs pressed against the wall, hearts pounding. Karl was right. We shouldn't be here. A bit late for second thoughts though. The hall to the left is lined with doors. The crew's cabins. All the doors are open, everyone is either in the lounge or working. But one door is closed.

"Penelope?" Karl whispers.

Only one way to find out. Lightly, I tap my knuckles against the door. "Penelope?"

No answer.

"Try again," whispers Karl.

"Penelope? Can we talk to you?" I knock this time, loudly. The door clicks open from the force of my hand.

It's quiet.

I peek in. "Penelope?"

The tiny bed is a mess of rumpled sheets. There's a desk with a small laptop. A wastebasket spilling over with tissues.

But no Penelope.

Karl nudges passed me and steps inside the little room.

"Karl," I hiss, "get out of there. You're going to get caught."

"Ridge, look," he says, standing by the desk. He's unfolding a piece of paper—a map. "I know these sites."

"What?" I join him by the desk, looking down at the map in his hands.

"See these red circles?" he says. "Penelope has marked up the map to line up with the chart on her computer." He points at a graph on the screen. Bold print across the top of the graph reads *Electromagnetic Anomolies*.

"I don't get it."

"These spots on the map," Karl says, "are shipwreck sites."

My eyes roam over the room. It's a mess. But it's...it's wrong. Chaotic. Like Penelope left in a hurry. My palms begin to sweat. "We should get out of here," I say. "Before she comes back."

Karl ignores me. He's bent down, inspecting a couple of framed photos on the desk.

In the moonlight cast by the porthole window something glints on the floor. I pick it up. It's Penelope's meteorite. "Karl..." I say, holding up the stone.

He frowns. Then he holds up the pictures he's been studying. "Check these out." The photos are black and white. Different crews going back decades. And Penelope smiling in each one.

"How is that possible?" I ask.

"I don't think they're all Penelope," Karl says.

"What do you mean?"

He shrugs. "I think that's just what they look like. Or more like what they dress themselves in. Sort of like…a uniform. They all look the same."

Sweat is drenching my hands. The meteorite digs into my palm. "*They?*"

"The aliens."

Suddenly we hear voices in the hall.

"What do you mean she's missing? When did you see her last?"

I jump on Karl and cover his mouth. Someone's coming. A man.

"I left her in her cabin after breakfast," says a woman. It's Dana. "She said she wasn't feeling well.

But when I came to check on her before dinner service, she wasn't in her cabin."

I scan the room for somewhere to hide.

"How do you know she wasn't in the bathroom?" asks Captain Bob.

"I've checked a few times," Dana replies. "I'm telling you, she's not here."

I press my back against the wall, pulling Karl with me.

But it's no use.

"Penelope?" Captain Bob knocks on the open door. He steps into the room and jumps at the sight of me and Karl. He notices the necklace in my hand. "What the...? What are you doing in here?"

Before I can think of an answer, the boat shutters. The tremor is so violent, I nearly fall over.

There's something wrong with the *Paradise II*.

Chapter Ten

Karl and I sit on the deck, pink morning sun glittering off the sparkly sea. There's a couple of bagels and fruit on a plate between us. Neither of us have touched them. My stomach is in knots, the couch practically vibrating from the symbol I know is painted beneath it.

The sea is calm, like an endless desert of glass. Everything is eerily quiet, except for the gentle lapping of water against the hull—and the murmurs of serious voices on the deck above. Captain Bob wasn't mad that Karl and I were in Penelope's room. At least, he never said so. Not even after I handed over Penelope's necklace. I thought he'd accuse us of stealing. But he didn't. When the boat shuddered, Captain Bob forgot us completely. He left us with Dana and hurried to the bridge to see what the problem was. Dana brought us back to our room, and Karl and I were told to go to sleep. Neither of us did. But we didn't talk either. I stared at the ceiling all night, thinking about Penelope, about what could be wrong with the ship.

Turns out, there's a lot wrong. At breakfast, Captain Bob announced that the ship's engines had failed. Not only that, but Penelope was officially missing. A rib, which is ship-talk for a little boat that takes people ashore, was gone. Since then, the adults have been in a frenzy of activity. The *Paradise II* is adrift, with no way of reaching shore.

Ash paces in front of us, her eyes swollen and puffy. She's been crying all morning. "We're going to die here," she says. "You can't drink seawater, you know? What happens when we run out of water? We'll dry up, that's what! Shrivel up like mummies!"

"Ash—" I try.

"Or maybe we'll drown," she says, voice hitching. "What if a major storm comes, you know? And we can't move? The ship could sink! I'm good at treading water but I can't do it forever."

"Ash!" I bark.

She looks at me, red-rimmed eyes blinking.

"You heard what Captain Bob said," I tell her. "They're going to radio for help. Someone will come and pick us up. You're not going to drown."

"But then why," she says, clasping her hands together, "haven't they told us when help is coming?"

I don't know how to answer that. Captain Bob made it sound like help was just a phone call away. We'd been at a standstill for hours. Shouldn't someone already be on their way to rescue us? Why hadn't Captain Bob announced that someone was coming?

Because of Penelope?

She was missing. That awful word had been echoing through my mind since Captain Bob had said it at breakfast. If she had taken the rib, where was she going? Why hadn't she contacted us to let us know she was all right? I remember the weight of the cool little stone in my palm. If she had left voluntarily, why would she leave her necklace behind?

The knots in my stomach tighten. What if she's not all right?

Looks like Captain Bob and the other adults have decided to send out a search team. I glance over the side of the boat. There's another rib being launched into the water by the first mate and the engineer. Captain Bob circles nearby on a jet ski, waiting for the boat.

"They're not going to find her."

"Karl!" Ash and I snap.

"What? It's true!" he says. "She doesn't want to be found. She's gone to find *them*."

"Find who?" asks Ash. "What is he talking about?"

Karl jabs his index finger into the couch, pointing at the symbol we both know is under there. Images from my dream flash across my mind—nuclear green glow, shadows beneath the waves. I shiver.

"Ash, honey?" Jes appears in the doorway to the dining room. Mom's beside her. The two of them are pale. "Can I talk to you?"

Ash gulps.

Something is wrong.

Well, something *more*.

Jes and Ash head into the ship. When they're gone, Mom takes a seat beside me on the couch. She takes my hand in hers but doesn't say anything. She's watching Captain Bob and the rib getting organized in the water. She runs a finger along her bottom lip, like they're chapped. She always does that when she's thinking hard about something.

"Mom?"

She turns and looks at me, squeezing my hand. She smiles a sad smile and then notices Karl for the first time. "How are you boys doing?" she says. "Are you okay?"

No, obviously we're not okay. "Mom," I say, "what's wrong?"

But she doesn't get the chance to tell me. Because just then there's a bloodcurdling scream from somewhere inside the boat.

Ash comes running out of the dining room, gulping down air, and leans over the side of the ship. "They can't call for help!" she wails. "The communication's busted too! We really are going to die out here!"

The tightness in my gut radiates all the way down to my feet. My hand clutches to Mom's.

We're stranded. In the middle of the ocean.

Karl jumps up, hands buried in his hair.

"We're going to be okay," Jes is telling Ash. "Everything is going to work out."

"Ridge," Mom says. Her tone is firm. It's the same one she uses when I'm in trouble. The one that demands I pay attention. It brings my senses into focus. "Captain Bob has assured Mr. Barrington that the situation is under control. Our itinerary is with the port in Nassau. When we don't arrive, they will know we've run into trouble. They will come and get us."

I want to believe that. I know she believes that. But all I can think about is the green glowing water from my dream. The shadow beneath the waves.

And Penelope.

"What is that!?" Karl has wandered all the way to the ship's bow. He's pointing into the distance. We hadn't really noticed that a heavy fog had rolled in.

When I jog up to join him, I barely can see what he's pointing at through the haze. Something is there though, shimmering like a mirage. It's another ship. But it's resting at an angle, like it has run aground. The jet ski and the rib are approaching.

Mom joins us, squinting into the distance. "Where the heck did that come from?"

It's a good question. I've paced this deck a few times in the last couple hours. I swear it wasn't there before. And even if it was, wouldn't Captain Bob have seen it?

"The hull," Karl squeaks, his voice strangled in his throat. "Ridge, look at what it says on the hull."

My knees feel like they're going to give out. Because painted on the ship's hull in bold black calligraphy is the one word I didn't want to see. *Paradise.*

Chapter Eleven

I haven't left the front of the boat all day. I sit at the bow, alone on the edge of the deck, arms draped over the railing. I can see Captain Bob's jet ski and the search team's rib. Tiny little specks parked on the distant shoal. There has been no movement for hours.

I hear the sound of soft padded feet on teak behind me. Karl sits down, his tablet, a notebook and felt marker in his hand.

I lean back on my hands. "What's taking so long?" I ask. "The ship's not that big. Why haven't they found Penelope yet?"

Karl shrugs. "I told you, they won't find her. She's gone."

"Come on, Karl."

"She has. She's gone to find the pilgrims."

I frown. "Aliens..." For some reason, I'm back to being skeptical. Must be the daylight.

Karl nods. Then he hands me the marker. "Take this."

I take it and he opens up his notebook. On one of the pages is the symbol Penelope painted under the couch. The symbol carved into the meteorite necklace. Karl has drawn it and redrawn it dozens of times, as best he can. The lines overlap, and the distances between them are inconsistent. "I can't make it look right," he says. He shoves the book at me, and turns on his tablet. The website with the symbol is on the screen. "You're good at drawing. Can you try?"

It's simple enough. I had drawn it before, that night on the deck. I barely have to look at the tablet. Three S's, laid on their sides, and three dots above them.

When I'm done, Karl takes back the notebook. There's a knot between his brow as he inspects my doodle. Finally he nods, satisfied. Then he pulls up his shirt sleeve. "Okay, now draw it on me."

"What?"

"Remember the article?" he asks. "*Mark yourself.* That's why Penelope drew the symbol on the deck. I'm not taking any chances." He shifts closer to me, holding up his sleeve.

"What do you think happened?" I ask him as I carefully draw the symbol on his skinny arm.

"I think Penelope is trying to go home. That's why she came here. That's why she marked the deck of the boat. To help the ship pass through the electromagnetic field. She's trying to follow the road to the gate."

I stop. "What gate?"

"The one at the end of Procyon's Road. The gate that will lead her home."

I rub a hand over my face. This is insane. Aliens and space gates? I look out at the wreck of the *Paradise*. An uneasy feeling wriggles in my gut. The *Paradise* is no bigger than the *Paradise II*. It shouldn't be taking this long to search the boat. None of this makes any sense.

Karl blows on the drying ink. Then he elbows me. "Now you."

I pause. I'm not actually going to draw this weird symbol on my arm for protection, am I?

Not taking any chances. A little voice is telling me to listen to this kid.

With a sigh, I draw the mark on the inside of my forearm. "So if Penelope's gone," I say, still trying to understand, "why is all this still happening? Shouldn't the boat have come back online when she got through the gate?"

"What do you mean?" asks Karl.

"She wouldn't just leave us stranded in the middle of the ocean forever."

I can't believe she would do that. Penelope isn't that kind of person. If she left to find her way back to wherever she comes from, then she would have made sure we could make it through the electromagnetic field safely without her. Wouldn't she?

Karl thinks for a minute. He picks at the corner of his notebook. "Maybe something happened."

"What?"

"Maybe she's in trouble," he says, grimly.

My gut clenches. What kind of trouble?

Before I can imagine an answer, there's a crash in the dining room. We wait, expecting to hear someone call out—Mom, Mr. Barrington, Jes, Dana. Anyone to explain the sound. But it's quiet. Weirdly quiet. It makes me wonder. How long has it been this quiet?

I leap to my feet and run toward the sound. Karl behind me does his best to keep up.

It's Ash. She's standing by the buffet table, broken juice glasses on the floor around her. Juice drips from the table onto the ground and pools around her bare feet.

"What happened?" I say.

But Ash doesn't answer. She just stands there, juice glass in hand. It's like I haven't said anything.

"Ash?" I wave a hand over her eyes. She looks just like Mom did—blank face, seeing nothing.

"The symbol," Karl breathes. "Ridge, give her the symbol!"

I look down at my hand. I'm still holding the marker. Quickly, I scribble the mark onto her arm.

When it's done, I step back. "Ash?"

She doesn't move.

"We're too late," says Karl.

No. He can't be right. We're fine. We're wearing the symbol, and we're completely fine.

Unless whatever did this to Ash came after…

I glance out at the ocean. The water around the boat is glowing.

Nuclear green.

My twisted stomach wrenches so violently, I nearly puke. *Mom.*

I take off running for her room. Karl shouts after me. The door is open. The bed is made. She's not here. I scramble down the hall and nearly run into Dana and Andres.

They're statue still, Andres holding out his hands like he's counting items on his fingers. But he doesn't move, just like Ash. Dana is holding a clipboard and pen like she's about to write something. But she isn't even looking at it. She's looking at nothing. It's like being in a wax museum.

My heart hammers in my chest. This can't be happening.

"Dana?" I shout, waving my hands in front of their faces. "Andres? Hello?" No response. I shake Andres by the arm. But still his eyes don't focus.

I race for the stairs to the upper decks, to the bar upstairs where the grownups like to hang out. And there's Mom. She's standing with Jes. They're facing each other, but their eyes are blank. Mr. Barrington and Gina are on the couch, their faces just as blank.

Karl arrives at the top of the stairs. He's breathless. "Dad?" he gulps.

Karl sits down beside his father, grabs his face in his hands. "Dad!" He snaps his fingers.

Mr. Barrington doesn't move.

No one does.

There's an ice bucket sitting on the coffee table. Meltwater filled to the top. I barely have enough time to dump the bucket before I hold it to my face. I puke.

This is bad.

I stare out at the green water. It's just like my dream. How can it be just like my dream?

"Ridge," Karl squeaks. "Ridge, what do we do?"

I remember Penelope. The way she was in my dream. The meteorite necklace she gave me. The feel of her kiss on my cheek.

The necklace.

She doesn't have it with her.

"We have to find Penelope," I say.

"But Captain Bob," says Karl, "he and the others still haven't come back."

"And he isn't going to," I say. Because Captain Bob doesn't wear the mark. Captain Bob doesn't know what we know.

Penelope needs her necklace.

And it's up to us to bring it to her.

Chapter Twelve

"Do you know what you're doing?" Karl frowns as I climb aboard the second jet ski. It's parked on a small floating dock, connected to the ship. The green glow of the water lights everything radioactive. It's creepy and unsettling. And it's making me want to go hide under the covers of my bed. I sit and stare at the controls. I have never ridden a jet ski before. Let alone driven one. I squeeze the key in my hand. Where do I put it?

The key was easy enough to find. Captain Bob kept it hanging on a row of hooks in the bridge. Right beside Penelope's necklace. The necklace now hangs around my neck, heavy and cool.

"Ridge?" says Karl, impatiently.

"No, Karl," I snap. "I have no idea what I am doing, okay?" I don't mean to bark at him, but what does he want from me? I don't know anything about private cruises, and pleasure crafts. And I definitely don't know anything about secret alien space gates and the women that go looking for them. But I'm trying. And it would be a lot less stressful if Karl would stop looking at me like I'm useless.

He points at a hole beside the steering controls. "That's the ignition."

I plug in the key and nothing happens. "Great. Now what?"

Karl points to a button beside the key that says *Start*. When I push it, the machine rumbles to life. Embarrassed, I glance sideways at Karl. He doesn't say anything, just hands me a life jacket. As I put it on, my palms begin to sweat. What are we doing? How exactly am I supposed to help Penelope? Save the ship? I can't even get the jet ski to work. If Karl is thinking the same thing, he doesn't let on. He unties our lines and climbs onto the seat behind me.

There's a bang as I ram the bumper into the dock. "Whoops," I say.

Karl taps my left arm. "Reverse," he says.

When I've got the hang of it, we head away from the ship. Ahead of us, we can see the *Paradise* up against the shoal. I can't help but feel like I'm heading toward a graveyard.

Karl points over my shoulder, "Pull up there!" Captain Bob's jet ski and the rescue boat are pulled up onto the shoal, tucked in just against the *Paradise*. And the rib, the one that went missing earlier—Penelope. I glide in beside them, the bottom of the jet ski scraping against rock. I wince, hoping I didn't just break a twenty-thousand-dollar water craft. Then again, if I somehow manage to save everyone, maybe Mr. Barrington won't mind.

Karl hops off, landing ankle deep in seawater. "Captain Bob?" he calls out.

There's no answer. All we can hear is the lapping of waves against the boats.

"Bob?" I try, hopping off. "Penelope? Are you in there?"

I stare up at the *Paradise*. There's algae and barnacles growing on her hull. I swallow, thinking about the people that were lost so long ago. Are they still on there? What's left of them anyway? I really don't want to climb aboard and find out. But I know that if Bob is anywhere, he's on that boat.

"Ridge?" says Karl. "Is this what's going to happen to us?" He nods toward the *Paradise*, broken and decaying on the shoal. I hope not. Not if I can help it. And that's when I notice it—a ladder, hanging off the starboard side.

"That must be where they climbed aboard." I take a step toward it, but Karl grabs my arm.

"Ridge, look," he says, pointing at the stern. In black painted ink is Penelope's symbol. She was here all right. I reach for her necklace, hanging from my neck. I hope Karl's right about the symbol being for protection.

"We better go check it out," I say, but Karl doesn't let go.

I try to pull my arm away, but he holds on tighter. His skin is pale, the color draining into his feet. "Bob," he says, voice practically a whisper. My eyes follow his, up past the symbol to the top deck.

And there he is. Bob. Still as a statue, staring out to sea.

"Bob!" I call out. But he doesn't flinch. Just like Ash. Just like Mom. And the others.

"We have to help him," I say, pulling my arm away from Karl.

"Ridge, wait!" calls Karl. But there's no time. If Bob is frozen like that, then it's safe to say the rest of the rescue team is on the ship too, frozen just like him. And I have Penelope's necklace. I touch the pendant at my neck. If I have it, then even she might be frozen, just like everyone else.

I plunge through the water, up to my knees, stumbling my way along the shoal. I'm nearly at the ladder when the sea begins to bubble and froth around me.

Karl screams, and the rocky shoal begins to shake beneath my feet. The pendant hanging from my neck feels hot, and when I look down it's glowing—green and bright, just like the water.

The water surges, pulling me forward. I slam into the side of the *Paradise*. Karl cries out for me. And then the water rushes back, slamming me down on the rocks so hard the breath leaves my lungs.

Aching and bruised, I lie flat on the exposed rock. I look up, and see the water—it's rushing back and back and back. Away from the shoal, opening up in front of me and revealing the naked seabed. And the massive, perfectly square bricks stacked on top of it.

"Ridge!" Karl is lying on the rocks just to the right of me. He's coughing and sputtering. But finally he manages to croak out, "The road! We found the road!"

I struggle to my feet and stare out at the path stretching before me.

Procyon's Road. We found it.

But it's not over yet. I clutch the pendant. It's hot and buzzing against my palm.

I know what we have to do, to save my mom, and everyone else. We have to follow the road. And find Penelope.

Chapter Thirteen

Karl and I walk side by side, picking our way over Procyon's Road. Creepy-crawly bottom dwellers scurry away from us. The bricks that lie here—the bricks *they* laid here—are perfectly square and smooth. But the coral and barnacles that have grown on them are rough. Karl and I hold on to each other, as much to keep our balance as our nerve.

"I don't know what it's worth at this point," I say. "But you were right, Karl. About all of it."

Karl looks up at me. Surprised. And I realize I should have said it sooner.

"I'm sorry I doubted you," I add.

He thinks about it for a second. It's like he can't understand why I've said it. Maybe I didn't need to. But standing in the middle of the exposed ocean floor, on a road built by aliens, looking for an alien girl trying to return to some kind of star portal—I feel like I did.

"Thanks, Ridge," he says finally. I nod and take another step and he adds, "Are you sure we're doing the right thing?"

"What do you mean?"

"I mean, look at the *Paradise*. If we bring this meteorite to Penelope, how do we know we won't all end up just like the people that were on that ship?"

It's a good question. One I don't know the answer to. "We *don't* know, Karl," I tell him, honestly, "but I just have this feeling that Penelope is the key to all this. And I know that we will definitely end up like the *Paradise* if we don't at least try."

Karl thinks about that for a minute, and finally nods, falling in step beside me again.

The road appears endless. Nothing but brick and stone as far as the eye can see. Soon the *Paradise* is barely a speck behind us. If the water decides to rush back in, we'll be in real trouble. And even if it doesn't, I don't know how easy it will be to find our way back to the *Paradise*. How far are we supposed to go? I don't even really know what we're looking for. Do I really expect Penelope to just appear out of the blue?

The sky is getting darker. But it doesn't look right. It's gray, with a greenish hue. Billowing clouds cluster overhead. It looks more like a painting than real life.

Karl's voice calls my attention back to the road. "What is that?"

Up ahead the road ends abruptly. My stomach lurches. There's a wall. A wall of water. It rises up a hundred feet, rushing and spraying and thundering. For a second I think it's going to come crashing down. And we'll be swept away in the deluge. But it doesn't. It just keeps rushing upwards somehow. At the base of the wall are stones. Stacked on top of each other. Karl and I move closer. We can see that the stones have intricate images carved into them.

A part of me, the part that likes to draw, takes over. I forget about terror of the rushing water, the mystery of the road. All I can think about are the lines. "It's people," I say, taking a moment to admire the art. The style is unlike anything I've ever seen. The characters are made up of hundreds of lines swirling into themselves—thick lines, fine lines. Deep and shallow. All of them curling around themselves so that the lines could sink into forever—like a black hole. But still, they come together in such a way that they make clear figures. Men and women, old and young. They gather together in the center, beneath a sky of churning clouds. All of them sinking into forever.

"They're beautiful," I say. And then I take step toward them.

"Wait!" Karl pulls me back. "This is some kind of trick."

"What do you mean?"

"Like a booby trap. Look." He points to the bricks directly at our feet. They're different from the ones that make up the rest of the road. They have images on them, like the swirling figures ahead. And their color is different. Darker. Glinting with a bioluminescence. "Mark yourself as friend," Karl says to himself.

"But we did," I say, pointing to the mark on our arms.

"Mark yourself as friend, and you shall be seen as a true explorer," he repeats.

Again, Penelope's words echo in my head. "A true explorer can never be too careful." That's what she said that day on the bridge. I look up at the carving of people. On either side of the group in the center, there are men. Each has one foot behind them, planted firmly on a square. In front, their feet find nothing but empty space. Their arms flail around them. Their mouths gape in a silent scream. Karl is right. Like he's been right about everything. This is a trick.

I stare at the men's feet. And the stones before us.

"We have to step in the right place," I say, finally understanding.

"How do we know what the right places are?" asks Karl.

I look down at the pendant around my neck. And back at the stones on the floor. There's no real pattern. It's all just carved swirling lines, thick and thin, like on the wall. Only on the ground they don't seem to form anything. It's just beautiful swirls and spirals. Like a field of galaxies.

I stare at the people carved into the rock wall. They gather in the center, a swirling spiral circle framing them all. "That must be the gate," I say. "They're all passing through."

Above the gate, is a glinting star. And on either side of the gate, above the falling men, are two more stars.

I hold the pendant, inspecting the symbol. Three squiggly S's on their side. Three dots. No. Not dots. *Stars.*

"What did that website say?" I ask Karl. "About the three stars? Procyon, Sirius and…"

"Betelgeuse."

"But Procyon is the brightest of the three…" I study the star above the gate and the crowd of people inside. It looks strange, I realize, because it's not positioned in the centre. It looks just a bit off.

Too far to the right. I think of Wraith, and my drawing of Penelope. Of the way I placed the lines. Each one a decision. A choice. And on the ground, the swirls of lines begin to make sense. "We have to follow the light," I say. "The light of Procyon."

"What?"

"Look!" I say, pointing. "The thick lines, those represent where the spirals are in shadow. But the thin lines, that represents the brightest part, where the light from the Procyon star is hitting. Just like the line work in a comic! We follow the thin lines."

Karl frowns. "Are you sure about this?"

No. I haven't been sure about anything since we left the dock in Florida. But it's the only answer we've got.

Chapter Fourteen

I hold my breath and take a step. My foot comes down gently on the thinnest of the lines.

Nothing happens.

I step again.

The road holds firm.

I glance back at Karl and grin. He bites his lip and follows after me. "Only the thin lines," I warn.

As we get closer to the wall, rocks begin to tumble away. Beyond it, a light. Green and glowing, nestled right against the rising water.

And a figure.

Silhouetted in the light.

"Penelope?" I say.

And then Karl cries out.

I glance back. He has lost his balance. His left foot touches one of the thick lines that represent the dark. I can feel the ground begin to quake.

"Ridge…." he says quietly. He looks terrified.

The stone at his feet begins to crack. I lunge for him, pulling him to me just as the brick falls away. There is nothing there now but an endless gaping dark.

Karl clings to me, his breath coming in quick gasps.

"You're okay," I tell him. "We're nearly there."

He only nods. He is too shocked to speak.

"Stay close," I say. "And watch where you step!"

We make our way, as carefully as we can. The rock wall in front of us crumbles with every step we take.

Finally, as we place our feet on the last step before the wall, it crumbles completely. And my heart nearly stops.

"Ridge? Karl?" It's Penelope. She is sitting down, lit by a vivid green light, the spray of the water beyond it misting everything from the rocks to her hair. She looks sad. Like she's been crying. She stands up, surprised. "Are you really here?"

I pick my way over the crumbled stone and remove the pendant from around my neck.

She gasps. "My meteorite!"

"It was on the floor of your room," I say. "We thought you might need it."

Tears fall from Penelope's eyes. "I thought I had lost it. I was sure I had it with me. But when I got here…." She reaches for it, but when she does, my hands pull away.

I think of Mom, empty eyes staring at nothing. "Our parents," I say. "Everyone on the ship..."

Penelope frowns and looks away. "I'm so sorry, for what my leaving must have done to you all. I never thought..." Then she stops. She closes her eyes. "This was all supposed to be over before anyone even noticed."

"We noticed," Karl says behind me. "Were you just going to leave us to rot there, like the *Paradise*?"

I wince.

"No!" she says. "My brother, the one who came here on the *Paradise*, he did not pass the forefather's test." She looks at me then. "But you did."

I understand now. The Procyon pilgrim who came on the original *Paradise*...they didn't manage to figure out the lines. They must have been swept out to sea. And no one could unfreeze the *Paradise* after that.

"I had a feeling, when I called you, that you would be able to figure it out," she says.

My eyes grow wide. "The dream?" I ask. "You did that?"

She nods. "But I was afraid I might have been too late. How did you two manage to avoid the frozen state?"

I show Penelope the mark on my arm. Karl shows his.

She smiles warmly. "True friends." She holds out her hand for the meteorite piece. "If you would allow me, I would like to set this right."

"How do we know we can trust you?" Karl says.

Penelope looks up at the green glowing light. The gate. She sighs. "You cannot."

She's right of course. It's because of her that the *Paradise II* is stranded. Because of her my mom and everyone aboard are expressionless zombies. But as I watch her watching the light, the gateway to the world she comes from, I realize that she means it. She never meant for any of this to happen. She only wants to go home. And with our help, she can.

And I believe that she can set things right.

I hand her the meteorite. She nods and places the pendant around her neck.

"Thank you," she says. "You are a true friend, indeed."

The stone begins to glow, its light matching the gate. Penelope steps forward. Within the light I can see them—figures, milling behind it. Just like in my dream. Penelope's family. She glances back at me and nods, pressing her palms to the light. They disappear within it. And she steps forward. She's swallowed by the light completely, until she's gone. And it's only me and Karl left standing in front of the light.

It's quiet. A strange sort of quiet. Like Penelope took the sound with her to wherever she's gone.

"Now what?" asks Karl.

And just as he does, the light swells, so bright that I'm nearly blinded. The ground begins to shake.

The tremors are violent. Tossing me and Karl to the ground.

"Ridge!" Karl screams. "Ridge! What's happening?!"

I don't know. All I know is, everything was supposed to be set right. But this isn't right. The misty spray of water is heavier now. Like a terrible storm. And when I look up, I see the water. It's tumbling down like a mighty waterfall. The wall of water is collapsing.

"Karl!" I scream, and lunge for him.

And then the water swallows us both up.

Chapter Fifteen

A shrill screaming fills my ears. I gasp, bolting upright.

The big-screen TV blinks to life, showing the weather and the navigation map.

I'm in my bed. Back in the cabin I share with Karl.

Karl's already up. He's sitting cross-legged on the edge of his bed. "Are we dead?" he whispers.

There's a banging on the door. I leap out of bed and fling it open. Ash.

"Are you coming or what?" Ash snarls. "You guys have been sleeping forever. Mom won't let me go snorkeling without you two. And you are wasting my whole day!"

I laugh. I can't help it. I'm just so relieved to see her scowling face. I wrap my arms around her. "Ash!"

"Ew!" she screeches. "Get off me!" She shoves me back. "Just hurry up, all right? Or I really will tell Bob to leave without you. I don't care what my mom says."

"Your mom? She's talking?"

Ash cocks an eyebrow. "Of course she's talking. Why wouldn't she be talking?"

She has no idea what I'm talking about. No idea about the zombie state. "And my mom? Have you seen her?"

"Obviously!" says Ash, impatiently. "She's waiting on the deck just like everyone else. Karl, your dad says if you're not up there in two minutes he's going to toss your tablet overboard."

I can't believe it. She's acting like nothing happened at all. "What about Penelope?" I ask. "Is Captain Bob still looking for her?"

"Who's Penelope?" says Ash.

I look back at Karl. His mouth is hanging open. Penelope really did it. Just like she said she would.

"Hello!" shrieks Ash. "Earth to losers. Are you coming or what?"

"Okay, okay," I say, grinning from ear to ear. "We're coming, we're coming."

I close the door and look back at Karl.

"Did she say snorkeling?" he says.

I laugh. The map on the screen indicates that we have arrived in Nassau. Just like we were supposed to. We've made it through the triangle.

"I guess…" I say, my brain still struggling to process what's happening. "I guess we should get our bathing suits on? Seeing as how we're not dead."

Karl smiles. "Yeah…I can put the tablet away for one day."

We get changed and grab towels and flip-flops as fast as we can. And on my way out the door, I grab my sketchbook.

"Think you can teach me?" asks Karl. "To draw, I mean."

"Yeah, Karl," I say. "I can do that. If you promise to show me a few more of those websites of yours. You never know when they might come in handy."

Acknowledgments

Thanks to my longtime best bud, Jess, who took me on an adventure that inspired so much of this story. Thank you to my writerly pals Alisha Sevigny and Ainslie Hogarth for your tireless support on this writing journey and for always being there to read and help. Thank you to my editor, Tanya Trafford, for your wisdom and eagle-eye. I have learned so much working with you. And thank you to my family, for putting up with me when I'm in the writing zone.

READY FOR MORE?

Check-out these other great paranormal and fantasy reads.

Blue Jasper must enter a magical forest when his siblings are kidnapped by a Faerie king.

"Excellent…A fast-moving urban fantasy."
—*CM: Canadian Review of Materials*

Macy's discovery could change everything.

"A magical story of bravery, friendship, and little brothers."
—*School Library Journal*

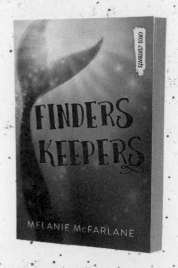

Swashbuckling
pirates rule the skies!

"A novel that jumps
off the page."
—*CM: Canadian Review
of Materials*

Xander and his friends
get in over their heads
during a role-playing
game in a supposedly
abandoned hospital.

"An immersive, page-
turning ghost hunt."
—*Kirkus Reviews*

M.J. McIsaac has a master's degree in writing for children and is the author of several books for young people, including *Boil Line* and *Underhand* in the Orca Sports line. She currently lives with her family in Whitby, Ontario.

For more information on all the books

in the Orca Currents line, please visit

orcabook.com